PROCESS

Ms H. Jama

TABLE OF CONTENTS

Chapter 1

Wind

Window

Gives us a second chance every morning,

So delightful,

Closes the curtain when we are mourning,

It is prideful,

Shadows us a night,

It can get frightful,

Sometimes it gets stuck,

It is spiteful,

Sometimes it is alone,

Idle.

Watching people zoom past,

Cycle,

Let's the light in the next morning,

Revival.

A winter Season

Violent wind circulates in the near distance.

Although tempted to act,

Instinct admits resistance.

72-hour rule,

In-case we add fuel

To the fire.

One half becomes livid,

As the thoughts are vivid,

The lack of clarity condenses the tension,

The cloud bursts into descension.

As the rain falls down,

The ground becomes soaked with transparency

Creating floods of sincerity

Anger simmers down,

They are allowed to be.

The cycle has ended, and they co-operate,

The sun shines again,

But resentment contaminates,

The floods evaporate,

Attempts to reconcile eradicate.

The cycle begins again,

Violent wind in the near distance.

Lotus Flower

The flower of rebirth

Always headed north,

Best petal forward,

Embracing the warmth,

That shines from the sky,

Even those that fly by,

Can smell the sweet and fragrant,

And you are always surrounded,

Never vacant.

Living through any extreme climate,

You survived the ice age

You're instinct is stronger than any primate,

Although,

The Yangtze River overflow,

But that was 1954,

And we don't believe in extinct no more,

Which is why you came back,

And forth is where you always go.

Beauty rising out of mud,

As you should!

Blossoming in different types of soil,

You are our moisture, the earth's oil.

So resistant to the pollution,

You are an infusion,

Of pesticides.

Suitcase

Ran away with you,

Flew with you,

And when my items consumed you,

I sat on you,

Cause the zip wouldn't close.

I suppose, you propose that I should stay home,

But you can't impose, cause you're so filled with my clothes.

And who knows?

One day I might agree with your opposing opinion

And you and I have always been one,

Some would say you are my companion,

Nah, you're one in a million,

Lockdown wouldn't let us be gone,

It made me forget, that you are my day one.

Just me and my suitcase,

You took me to the plane,

Oh, how insane, it was to obtain

All that you contained,

And my hand will always strain,

Cause you are too heavy,

When I push you on the trolley.

I'm gonna stop now,

Cause I could talk forever on how

My suitcase

Blue mixed with orange

Blue mixed with orange,

The combination is foreign,

Green in the near distance, brown in the far corner,

Surroundings turn into a border,

Eyes close and no one has seen or heard her.

Unknown is where they prefer,

Her.

Then they try to merge her,

Blue mixed with orange,

The combination is foreign,

Turquoise blankets cover half the planet,

And it,

Brings us peace,

Unless they rise,

And fall on the sand,

Pushing us back to the land.

Blue mixed with orange,

The combination is foreign,

You ever tried to make sense of something uncommon?

Like sense is the default,

And it's our fault,

That we think patterns is the norm,

When all they are is a repetitive form, Blue mixed with orange.

Low maintenance friendships (LMF)

Only see you once in a while,

Cause when madness happens in our lives, we have each other on speed dial.

This life has got us caught up,

And when we finally spoke, you told me how your ex was corrupt,

I was shook,

And then mid-convo my phone rings, interrupt Low maintenance friendships,

I'd always recommend this,

One of life's best things,

It transcends the rings

Of high maintenance friendships.

That keep you in a circle, expecting so much.

Entitled is the word for such.

Anyway,

A low maintenance friendship,

My favorite thing in the world,

Don't want to end it.

Even if we haven't seen or heard,

From each other,

And its' beautiful cause' we never complain,

Even when we struggle to sustain Contact,

Cause the love is always there,

And we understand, there is never despair.

A quick Autumn

Trees' shedding by the intensity of the breeze,

Footsteps then break those crispy leaves.

Gloomy fog deceives,

The animals in the distance,

That hide behind the trunk weaves,

Weather headed in minus degrees

Summer leggings have become autumn jeans,

So my legs don't freeze,

Enroute to the local coffee shop to receive some expertise,

On their tastiest drink.

It's a quick autumn,

The season that taught them,

Loss.

Autumn always seems to go by so quickly,

So, still she,

Couldn't comprehend the half days, merely,

Light at 5pm.

At this time of year, the streetlights become our hidden gem,

With equal distance between them,

They light up the November blues,

It's time to choose.

Which warm coat we will overuse.

It's quick Autumn,

The season that taught them,

Loss.

Sunday Morning/ Where did the weekend go?

Dogs barking in the near distance,

Errands calling, but energy has no persistence

To carry them out.

The Laundry is still not done,

Forcing myself to get out of bed,

For me, the weekend has just begun.

Saturdays are for getting over the week,

Sundays are preparing for the week.

I'm weak,

We actually don't have a weekend.

I'm still yawning,

Dish washer needs emptying,

And I haven't yet turned on the heating.

Would be insane to suggest a third day,

Maybe we should all fill out a government survey,

That wouldn't work anyway.

PM has arrived,

Getting in a warm shower before it's too late,

We are deprived,

Of a third day,

Much to my surprise,

It is now Monday.

Where did the weekend go?

A linguistic riddle

A group of words that contains a subject and a verb,

And I heard'

That they have a relationship.

Round of a clause.

Pause,

Reborn,

That's a language isolate,

Which means it evolved from a distance mate.

To make some noise,

Let's look at the IPA,

Have you ever tried to create a new sound or language?

Now that's a throwback essay.

Let's construct some shit

But what if they don't permit?

Cause prescriptivists have always loved to prohibit.

The minimal pair, making the fairest distinction

Differ in one element,

But there are two fictions.

Always looking for entailment,

But finding a presupposition,

Because I never know truth condition.

Dual Carriage Way

Two paths, one road,

Each one showed,

A different code,

& if we drove -

Too slow it would explode.

So, it's time to unload,

The hopefully decode.

Two paths, one road.

I found that the one thing we love, is the same thing we hate,

The one thing that makes us great,

Is the same thing that can break,

Us down,

Dual carriage way,

Feels like a Tuesday,

If you know what I mean,

I mean,

The fall makes us high,

And I don't know why,

I would be lying if I attempt to deny,

That sometimes your ego can be your friend,

Other times it brings you to an end.

Silent Sounds

It is silent,

But it is also a sound,

Frequency stay's in between 20Hz and 20,000Hz,

Anything exterior is renowned,

Silent sounds humans can't perceive is an infrasound.

However, some sounds are not obvious though we hear them
frequently,

I guess we have to be extremely, Observant,

To hear something that is the opposite of turbulent,

To recognise the permanent,

Miss.

Right earlobe is windy,

Whooshing so subtle but it is felt skin deep,

The Masseuse's hand recreates the sweep,

With their repeating movements.

Throat swallowing, or feet dragging,

Come after fingers typing,

The pause between the silence,

Is even more silent,

But this is also a sound,

Even if we don't hear it,

Quite literally,

Even with our ability,

The sound seems to be,

Unheard of.

Diffuser

Infuse the bad scent with a diluted mixture,

Oil base is a great structure,

Parting the dispute with an unknown vulture,

You can't fight fire with fire, so we added some water,

Fists still throwing shots, so we increase the manual instructor.

Temporary fix, the rampant particles are still heightened,

But the scent has weakened,

This is enough to call it truce,

But the love has unsweetened.

Patient enough to see it through,

But the lack of understanding has deepened.

Temporary fix, diffuser is limited,

Losing its power we change the base,

From rosemary to fragrant almond.

But we still have a bitter taste.

No amount of diffuser will erase.

This won't fail, we serve face,

But the diffused air starts to escape,

Panting for victory both move to a different headspace,

Wanting to turn off the diffuser and face,

The truth,

But the packet hasn't finished it's time to try grapefruit.

Sun/Boundaries

Not solid but stays in the atmosphere,

Surrounded by 8 imperfect spheres,

147.14 million km from here,

It has set boundaries with us,

Because it can kill if we get too close but, Warms us-From the right distance,

So, there is no pretense.

We know what to expect,

But right now, it's too difficult to detect,

Because climate change has been added into the mix,

But we won't talk politics.

Sun,

It has set boundaries with us.

Love at first sight

Rose lemonade by the sea front,

Toes dipped in the sand,

Time to confront,

What I have been craving,

Head titled star gazing,

Tote bag somewhere lying around,

Jhene playing in the background,

Right now,

Lover sat in front of me,

Dreaming of being loved unconditionally,

Without a time-stop,

No lease,

Just nonstop

The opposite of decease,

Like growing a field full of crops,

No need to talk,

Our hearts speak,

Don't want to leave this imaginary bubble, pop!

Chapter 2

Petunia

Isolation

A Complex-PTSD mind out of isolation is like a fish out of water,

But we are criminalized by the oversea yachter,

Overseeing - many replicates they misunderstood the nuances,

Judging the fish on his,

Decision to leave the water,

"How can they swim away from the element that helps them survive,"

Not all fish can enjoy the water, it's intense,

The water is so dense,

And the constant interaction with other fish is immense,

When the fish is out of the water,

It's a relief Yes human's need interaction cause' we are social creatures,

But isolation is a cure, beyond belief.

Rage

It all happens really quickly,

It's like

The breathe stops,

And her eyes pop,

She balls out with a sob,

Her hand is too heavy, and she ends up breaking the doorknob,

It doesn't stop,

Sweat runs downs her chest, while she tries to catch her Breath

Tightness makes her heart race faster,

Her mind won't stop the chatter,

She closes her eyes,

And to her surprise,

The rage dies,

And then things start to slow

Down.

The thoughts,

drown

Finally, she came,

Down.

Loss

I wasn't grieving the fact that we weren't in contact anymore,

I was grieving everything we could have been and more,

There was so many plans I had,

Just can't keep the good memories intact.

She really wanted to love you in your all,

Spend Saturday mornings at the stall.

She wanted to introduce her favorite dishes to your taste buds,

Laugh on the couch together in your warm fluffs.

Loss isn't just everything that it was,

It's the feeling of accepting what it won't be,

Tracing the steps of how things came about,

Overthinking, trying to see,

How everything got so sour,

How we reached the final hour.

Hate is Love

It is mean, but so amazing at the same time.

The way it confuses our black and white thinking should be a crime.

Grey area, confounds our tough exterior, Actions and words are non-linear,

Too much contradiction makes me weary of It.

The theory is that hate is love,

That has gone wrong,

The transfer of

Something prolonged.

In ourselves,

We see it.

Trust

Five applications –

One choice,

Five reservations booked

But only one receives the product.

Five adults,

One child,

Five people consult,

But there is only one result,

Behind every door is another unexpected hide,

Hard drive,

Is a great solution, but we also add it to iCloud just in-case.

Everything gets erased,

One is not enough,

I add another four just for back-up.

Trust is on 5 to one,

'Just in-case' entrenched in my mind,

There is always something to replace,

Just in-case.

Chapter 3

Lilac

Nails

New month new colour,

Let's rule out the ones that look duller, Ah! How about multicolor,

Reminds me of the summer,

When it's time to choose I stutter,

A small buffer,

And I chose brown.

Fleece

They're so warm,

But not too heavy,

They comfort us in the storm,

But don't make us sweaty,

They're so soft,

But not too thick,

We all have one in hiding in the loft, Grab it, quick!

They're all so different,

But not to individual,

On our bodies they are liniment,

Almost mythical.

Coffee

Fell in love with you when I worked at Starbucks,

And I only drank from the reusable cups,

Gave those city workers their drugs,

Intrigued how it make everyone chuck,

I took a look.

When I drank it,

I was hooked!

Depending on the weather,

I decide whether,

It's the Iced Mocha, or Latte and crème mixed together.

Having it in Cake or Tiramisu,

Reminds me again,

Coffee is you.

Sweater

Crewneck or turtleneck?

I'm not sure.

Double collar or Dad collar?

How about all four.

Sweaters.

Depop or vinted?

Apparently any marketplace is minted,

With sweaters.

Old school branded ones,

Ha, I want tons!

Of sweaters.

Black Vans

Some say basic,

I say my bare necessity.

The plain black is so mosaic.

My favorite accessory.

You slide on so easily,

I forget the need to be,

Because you dim down the complexity.

And walk with me in solidarity.

I love the care you have for me, I love changes,

But you protect me.

Longevity, there's no ages.

Underwear

High briefs for a bloated day,

Granny ones for a period day.

Confidence booster,

Unless you get a wedgy,

Then you scream like a rooster.

A packet of 5 for 10 quid,

Bargain again,

Cause God forbid,

We ever spend more,

for underwear.

Thongs are for show,

Cause as soon as I sit down,

They are uncomfortable.

Feel good in them.

Just impractical.

Anyway, I love underwear,

Even when they tear.

Pictures

To live in the moment, or to capture the moment?

Never understood which one to go for.

Well,

I love the moment so much that I want to capture it.

I love the moment so much, that I want to live in it.

Dwell.

I can't pick, I Yell,

Well,

The moment has now gone.

Damn, I should have recorded it.

Tiramisu

5 components,

Which one is dominant?

Well, that depends on the moment.

The coffee wakes you,

The cream soothes you,

The lady fingers hold you,

Up tight.

The sprinkled chocolate showers you.

One mouth full.

Hair Oil

When we apply it, we have such a shiny face,

It can easily spill, so we keep it in a small plastic case,

Next to our silk wrap, we hide in the self-care space.

Yesterday I was sat listening to Big Latto, whilst I mixed the castor oil with avocado.

Each oil serves a different purpose,

The castor oil soothes the surface,

Of our edges.

Gosh I love hair oil!

We are so spoilt,

Sometimes we even get to wrap some tin foil,

On our head for a deep condition,

It is more than a self-care tradition,

This routine allows us to transition,

Into Something knew, a different view.

And after we apply it,

We run to the mirror to review.

The hair oil.

Chamomile

Every morning we put the herbal teas on trial, Green Tea looks too hostile,

And those insta' influencers make it seem as though this drink is something that keeps us in style.

What a pile…

Anyway,

It's chamomile,

I put on a smile,

While ….

Wait *changes the rhyme*

Damn Chamomile.

Chamomile tea,

Calms us down, like counting to three.

Good morning,

And the tea is scorching,

The throat is sourcing,

The jug is outpouring,

And one more thing,

It is absolutely rewarding,

The mood is softening,

This is what happens when we drink chamomile.

Tea of rest and relaxation,

Taken over the morning, invasion.

Perception

I'm Sat chewing on the plastics',

This poem is quite big on the semantics',

Depending on the context, pragmatics',

It's a Wednesday and the time is passing by,

At this time of night, the ocean gets covered in the dark blue dye,

Because midnight will soon arrive.

It's also autumn, so I can't see any hive.

Sat here trying to describe,

So many metaphors I've already tried to apply.

Outside the streets are empty because the city never sleeps,

Neither do the foxes,

That's why you see them gathering around heaps,

Of rubbish,

Leftover food is their wish,

I'm still sat here trying to distinguish.

The things we threw for,

Nothing.

Is another beasts,

Something.

Perception.

The ability to philosophize something in isolation.

Printed in Great Britain
by Amazon